For Mummy Bears everywhere ~ A R

For Jenny, the best big sister in the world,
and for our mum ~ A E

LITTLE TIGER PRESS
An imprint of Magi Publications
1 The Coda Centre, 189 Munster Road, London SW6 6AW
www.littletigerpress.com

First published in Great Britain 2009
This edition published 2010

A CIP catalogue record for this book is available from the British Library

Printed in China

2 4 6 8 10 9 7 5 3 1

Me and my Mum

Alison Ritchie

illustrated by Alison Edgson

LITTLE TIGER PRESS
London

Me and my mum
are together all day.
I follow her footsteps
as we go out to play.

We make strings of flowers
and Mum is so clever
That *her* daisy chain
seems to go on forever!

We roar in the cave
and it answers our call
With magical echoes —
one big and one small.

GRRR!

GRRR!

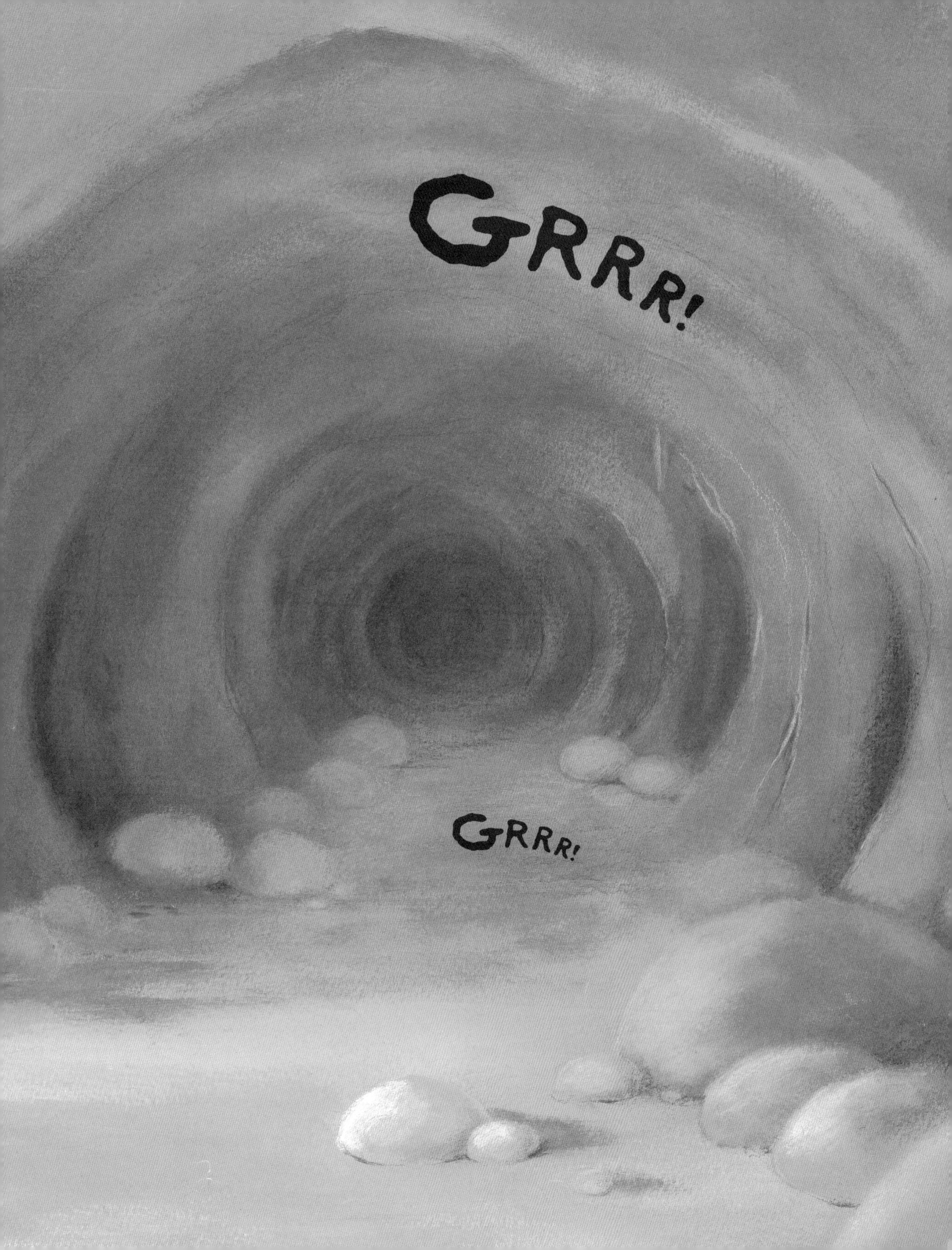
GRRR!
GRRR!

My mum's not afraid
of the dark or the night.
And I'm brave like her
when she's holding me tight!

We know a good trick,
my mummy and me –
I balance one apple
and Mum can do three!

The ice is so slippy –
it's easy to fall.
But soon, just like Mum,
I won't tumble at all!

We glide through the water
and I make a wish
That one day, like Mum,
I will swim like a fish!

With a showery spray
my mum dries her fur.
I wiggle my bottom
and shake just like her.

It's a long way to jump —
I'm not sure if I dare.
But I know I'll be safe
with my mummy right there!

We scoop up some leaves
and throw them up high,
Then watch as they float
gently down from the sky.

From my soft, furry ears
to the tips of my toes,
Mum says I'm the best little
bear cub she knows!

My mum is so special
in every way.
I want to be just like
my mummy one day.

More Little Tiger books for you and your mum to share

Time for Bed, Little One

Caroline Pitcher · Tina Macnaughton

Don't be Afraid, Little Ones

M Christina Butler · Caroline Pedler

I Love You, Sleepyhead

Claire Freedman
Illustrated by
Simon Mendez

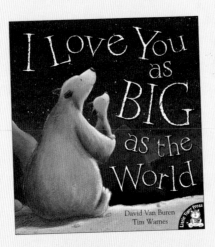

I Love You as BIG as the World

David Van Buren
Tim Warnes

Snuggle Up, Sleepy Ones

Claire Freedman
illustrated by
Tina Macnaughton

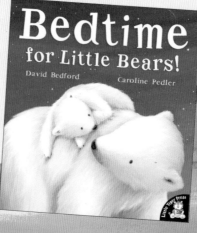

Bedtime for Little Bears!

David Bedford · Caroline Pedler

For information regarding any of the above titles
or for our catalogue, please contact us: Little Tiger Press,
1 The Coda Centre, 189 Munster Road, London SW6 6AW
Tel: 020 7385 6333 Fax: 020 7385 7333
E-mail: info@littletiger.co.uk • www.littletigerpress.com